Can you spot the Top hats through the book?
How many can you find?

I dedicate this book to all those children that have heard it in my dance classes,
and to those who are hearing it for the first time.
I hope you too have magic tap shoes.
Thank you to my family and friends for supporting me in this venture.

The Tap shoe story

Once upon a time there was a little girl who loved to dance.

She danced with the butterflies in the summer.

She danced with the snowflakes in the winter.

She danced in the wind and the rain.

But most of all she wanted
to go to a tap dancing
class with her friends.

She asked her mum

Please can I go to the tap dancing class

But her mum said...

"But whhhyyyyyy?" asked the little girl.

"Because tap shoes are too **NOISY** and they give me a headache!" said her mum.

The little girl was very sad and ran up to her bedroom and wept.

A fairy was flying past and heard the little girl crying.

The little girl was a very good little girl so the fairy was sad and asked

The girl said, through her tears, "I want to go to a tap dancing class with my friends, but my mum won't let me"

"Oh no, why not?"
asked the fairy

"She said that tap shoes are too **NOISY** and they give her a headache."

The fairy flew back to her fairy friends and told them all about the little girl.

"We must help her." they all said.

They got together and made
a magic potion, putting in
lots of ingredients.

Each fairy chose something special to
put in.

There was a
banana to help them
slide on the floor,

perfume to make them smell nice,

and some glitter to make them sparkle.

What would YOU add to the magic mixture?

Then they all added their
magic fairy dust

and gave it
one last stir

before dipping in a pair of tap shoes.

When they were dry, the fairy flew back to the little girl, carrying the tap shoes.

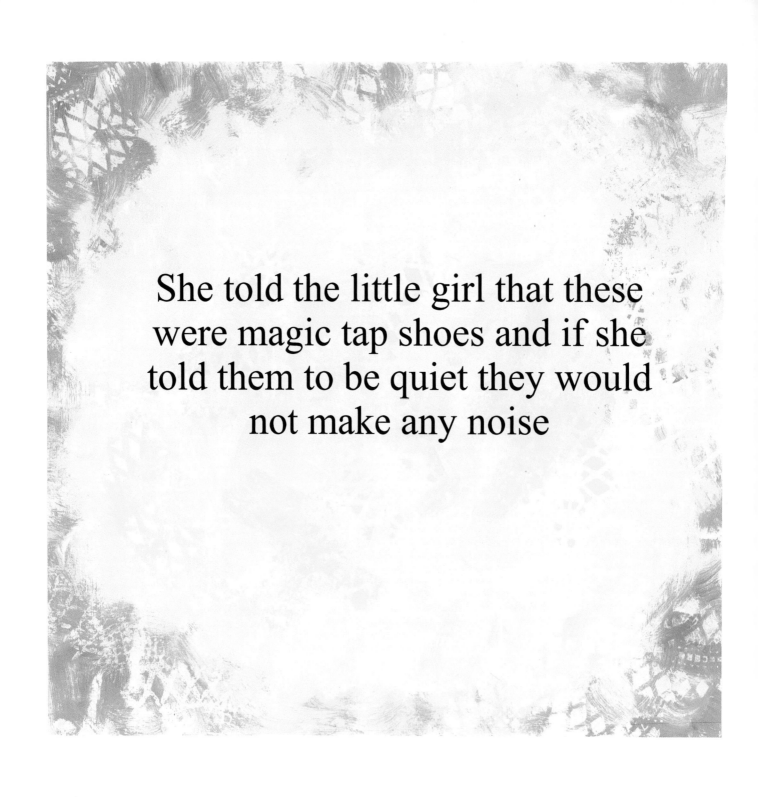

She told the little girl that these were magic tap shoes and if she told them to be quiet they would not make any noise

BUT

if she told them to be **NOISY**
they would make lots of great tap
sounds.

The little girl was so excited.

She thanked the fairy and then ran downstairs to tell her mum.

"WHAT?"

The fairies have brought me some magic tap shoes and they are quiet when you tell them to be so they won't give you a headache so they are only noisy if you tell them to be and they are ... tell them to be so they are quiet when you ... I go to the tap class now? please can I? Can I?

And her mum said….

And so the little girl got to go to her tap dancing class. She performed in shows and became a dancing star.

So, if you have a pair of tap
shoes that have a shiny bit
on the bottom then they just
might be magic tap shoes
too.

Test them out.

Tell them to be quiet and see if they can make no noise.

Tell them to be **NOISY** to see if you can make great tap noises too.

THE END

Printed in Great Britain
by Amazon